The Usborne Little Children's Travel Activity Book

James Maclaine

Designed and illustrated by

Erica Harrison, Benedetta Giaufret,
Enrica Rusinà, Laurent Kling, Mattia Cerato,
Lauren Ellis and Agostino Traini

Additional designs by Alice Reese

Edited by Fiona Watt

You'll find the answers to the puzzles
on pages 61-64.

On the road

Find the stickers for these pages in the middle of the book. Then, stick each one on top of the label it matches.

yellow taxi

green car

blue bus

vrroomm

red truck

moo

orange motorcycle

pink car

white van

zoom

quack

quack

blue car

red bicycle

beep

red car

purple car

3

Departures

There's lots to spot at this airport.
Can you find...

...3 luggage carts?

...2 passengers sleeping?

...a woman putting on her boots?

...a girl playing with a little car?

...3 striped suitcases?

...a boy playing with a toy plane?

...a girl taking photos?

5

Take the train

Complete the picture with a black pen.

Add wheels and windows
to the trains.

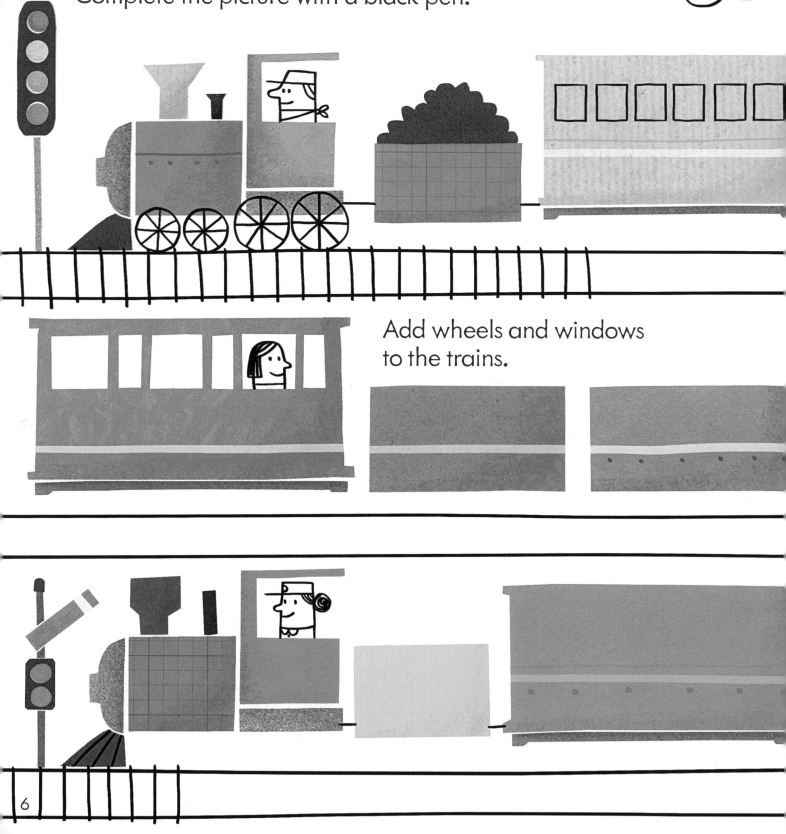

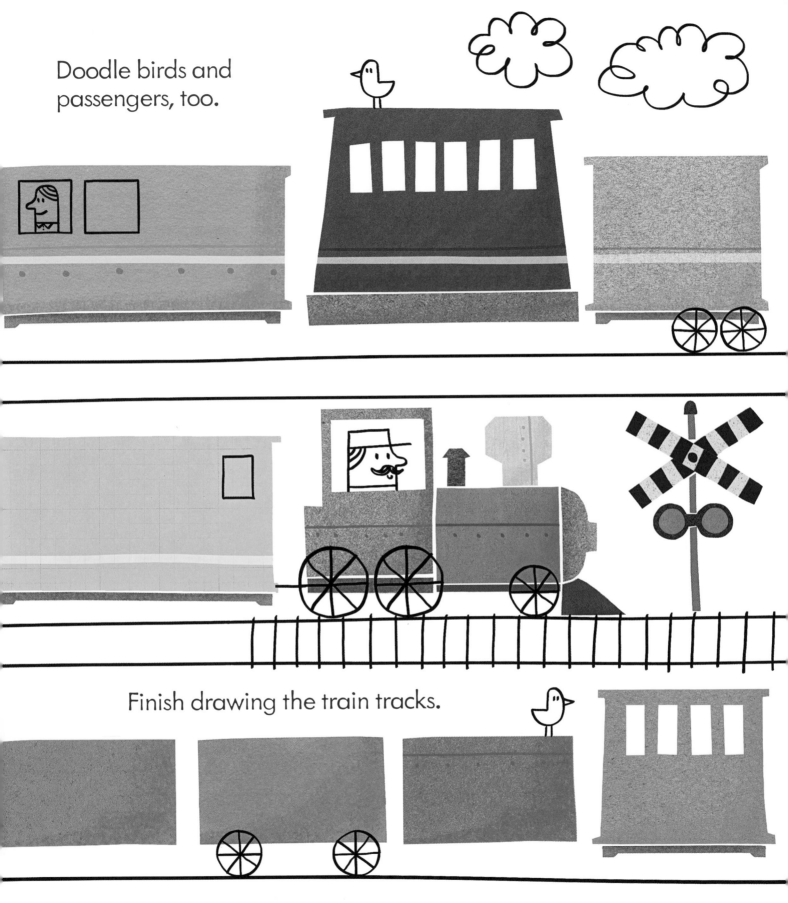

Doodle birds and passengers, too.

Finish drawing the train tracks.

7

On the beach

Connect the dots from 1 to 10.

5
4
2
3
6
7
8
9
1 10

You could draw flags on top, too.

Color the surfboards with markers that match the dots.

Draw over the dotted lines to finish the kites.

Which seagull is different? Circle it.

Snowy slopes

Count how many people are skiing and how many are snowboarding.

There are .... people skiing and .... people snowboarding.

How many animals can you spot enjoying the snow, too? ....

Draw a line leading the sled down the slope, passing around each of the flags from 1 to 10.

Give each snowman a face, some buttons and a hat.

Making camp

Find the red tent sticker on the sticker pages. Then, stick it on the map so it's...

- east of the lake
- west of the sheep
- and north of the trees.

Put the pictures in the order they happened.
Number them from 1 to 4.

Which RV is different? Draw a circle around it.

Jungle life

Color in the animals
on these pages.

Draw more black
stripes on the tiger.

Add more spots to the leopards.

At the market

The children are thinking about what they want to buy. Draw lines from the children to the stalls they need to go to.

Flora's Flowers

Vacation Hats

Baked today

Draw over the dotted lines in blue to finish the fountain.

How many pigeons
can you spot?   ....

Souvenirs

Ice cream

Summer Style

Fresh fruit

Making a splash

Draw a line as quickly as you can down the slide. Try not to bump into the sides with your pen.

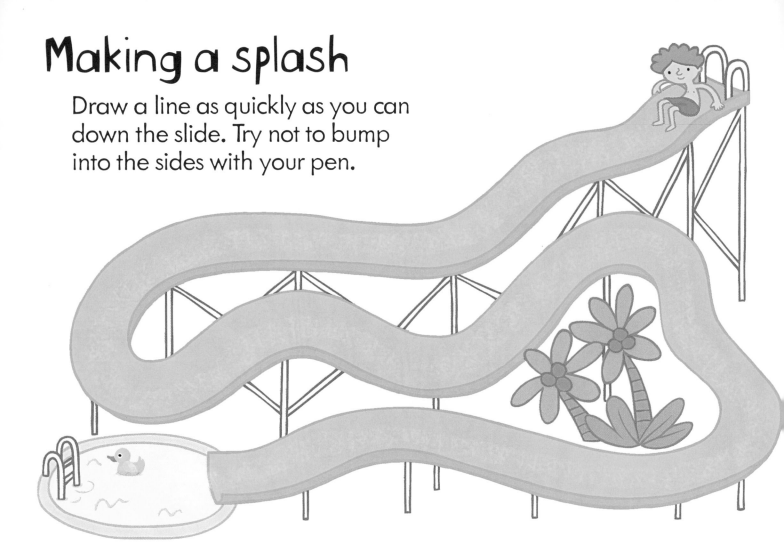

Which square completes this picture puzzle? ....

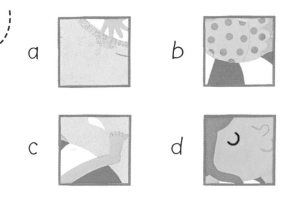

a

b

c

d

How many yellow ducks can you spot on these pages?

....

Color in the swimmers' suits to match their swimming caps.

Draw goggles on some of them, too.

Town travel

Read the bus route, then lead the bus around the town past all the places in the right order. Draw a line to show the way it goes.

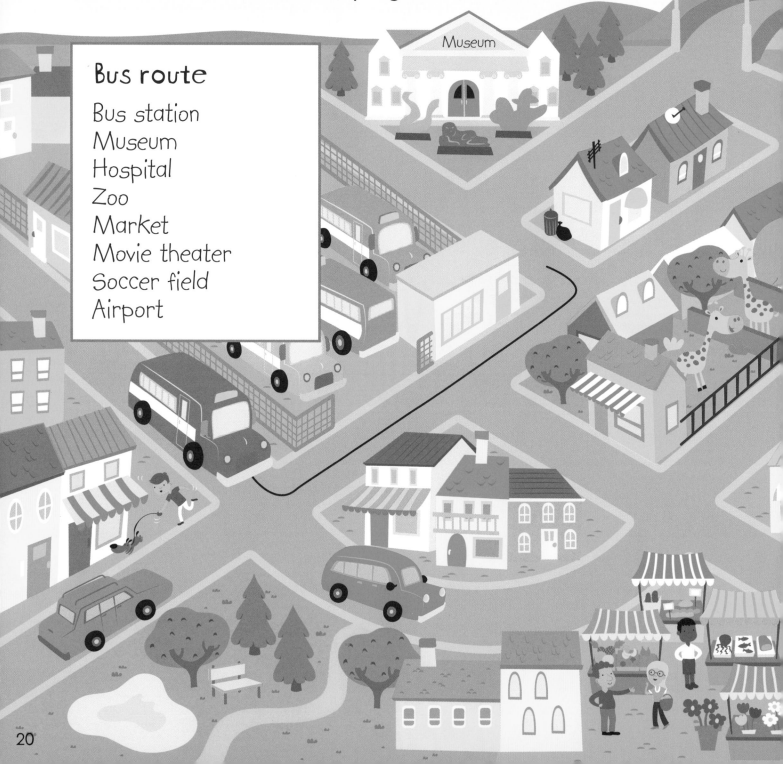

Bus route

Bus station
Museum
Hospital
Zoo
Market
Movie theater
Soccer field
Airport

Museum

Zoo

Movies

Usborne field

Up in the air

Can you find and color...

...2 spotted hot-air balloons?

...a jumbo jet?

whirrr

...2 striped planes?

whoosh

...a plane with 2 pilots?

...3 helicopters?

whizzz

...3 birds that aren't flying?

23

At sea

Draw a line between each pair of boats.

Which boat is the odd one out?

John Dory

Finn

Ray

Who has caught the most fish?

....

Can you spot the crab?

Packing

Can you help the children pack? Find the missing items on the sticker pages and stick them in the suitcases.

Follow the lines to find out where the three cars are going.

Read Harry's list and look at the picture. What is missing?
Draw a line under the word.

camera

teddy bear

candy

activity book

sunglasses

hat

Harry

Airport

Train station

Platform puzzles

Oh no! Simon has lost his ticket. Draw a circle around the ticket when you spot it.

Simon

Can you find Jack?

- Jack is on the train.
- He is wearing a T-shirt.
- He has curly hair.
- He likes to read.

Which girl is Jenny and which is Alex? Follow each speech bubble to find out.

Picture postcards

Follow the line without taking your pen off the paper.

Start here.

Paris

Adam Thompson
10 Station Road

Add more birds in the sky and boats on the sea.

Wish you were here

ving
time.
unny
nd
ool.
ach
nd
ater.
ere.
ica. X

Fill in the shapes with pens that match the dots.

LONDON

Connect the dots from 1 to 9.

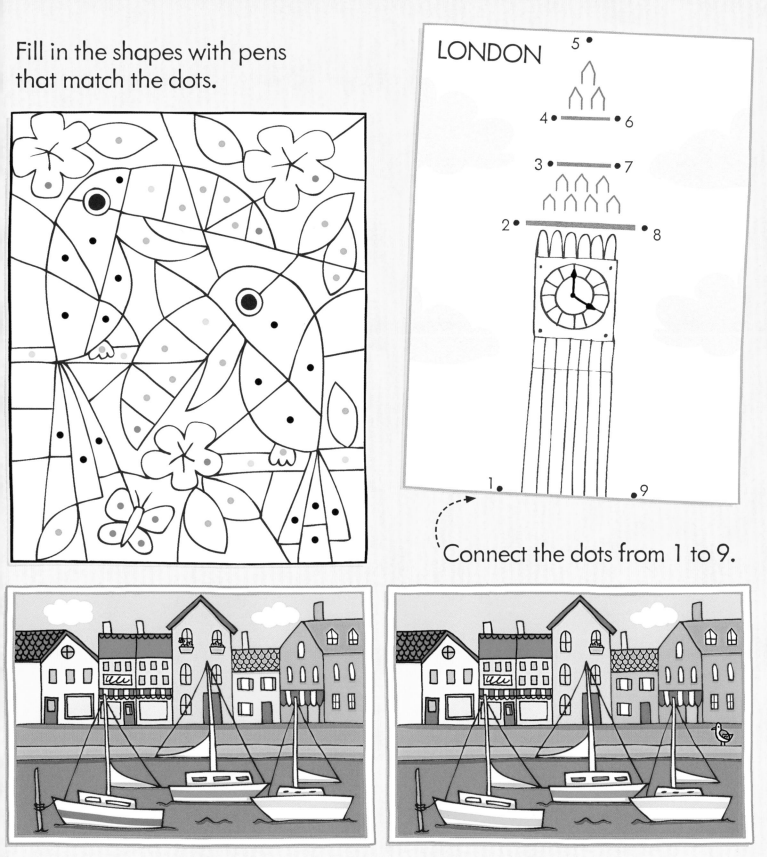

Circle the five differences between these two pictures.

31

Beachwear

Press on the stickers from the sticker pages to get these children ready for the beach.

On the road

Making camp

Packing

Beachwear

Harbor view

Time to eat

Travel fun
pages 56-57

Vacation pics
page 60

Under the sea

Doodle a face on each of the underwater creatures including the shells.

Pedal power

Can you spot...

...a dog?

...a tricycle?

...a black helmet?

...a bike with 2 people on it?

...a bike with a very big wheel?

34

Draw lines to join the cyclists with their matching helmets and bikes.

Which track did the boy's bike make? ....

To the train

Draw a line leading this man from the parking lot to the train.

How many clocks can
you find in the picture? ....

Draw a circle around each one you spot.

37

Harbor view

Match the building stickers to the shapes here and stick them on.

Can you guide this little tug through the maze of boats to the big red ship?

Look for a yellow submarine, too.

Airport arrivals

Can you spot five differences? Circle each one.

Whose passport photos are these?
Find the people in the line.

Can you help the passengers find their luggage?
Draw lines to show each one the way.

Tidepool hunt

Search the tidepool and the shore. Write the number of each thing you see below the pictures on the opposite page.

I can see...

4
....

43

On the move

Draw a line leading the plane through the clouds as quickly as you can.

Count how many red cars and how many blue cars are in the two long rows.

☐ red cars   ☐ blue cars

Draw hot-air balloons in the sky by following these instructions.

How to draw a hot-air balloon

Draw a balloon.

Add a basket.

Join both parts with lines.

Time to eat

Complete the meal. Draw...

...meatballs and spaghetti...

...fizzy bubbles...

...and watermelon seeds.

Put these pictures in the correct order. Number them from 1 to 3.

What's missing from the grill in picture b?

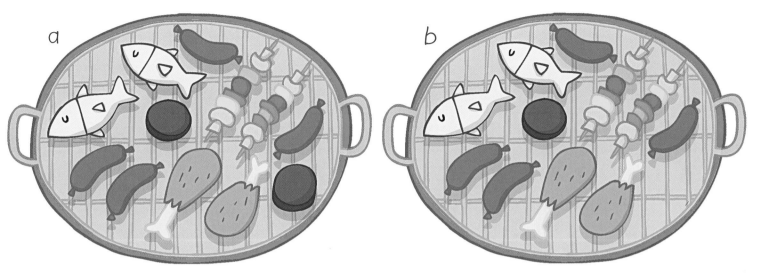

Add the ice cream stickers to give the children the flavors they want.

Strawberry

Mint choc chip

Vanilla

Chocolate

Where in the world?

New York

Los Angeles

Brasília

Santiago

Can you figure out where Anna is on the map?

She's in the square where there are...

- trees
- mountains
- and a lake.

Write her name in the square.

48

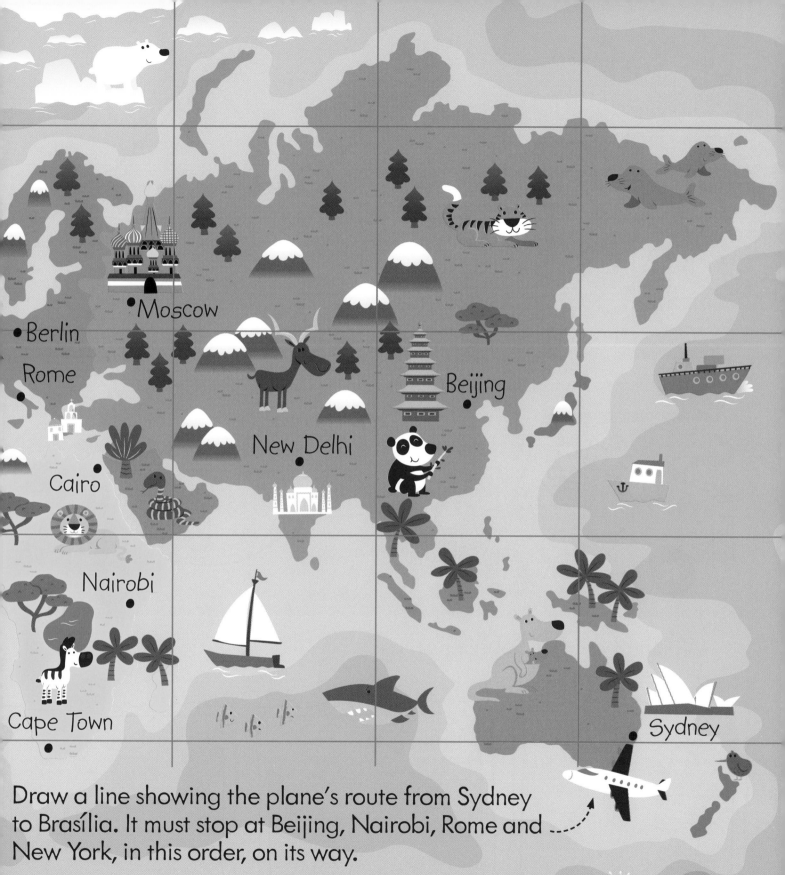

Moscow

Berlin

Rome

Cairo

Beijing

New Delhi

Nairobi

Cape Town

Sydney

Draw a line showing the plane's route from Sydney
to Brasília. It must stop at Beijing, Nairobi, Rome and
New York, in this order, on its way.

On safari

Sophie

Which photo has Sophie just taken? ....

a

b

c

Which zebra doesn't match?

Draw a curly mane around this lion's head.

Put the giraffes in height order. Label the shortest one 1 and the tallest one 5.

Space travel

Complete the picture with the space stickers from the sticker pages.

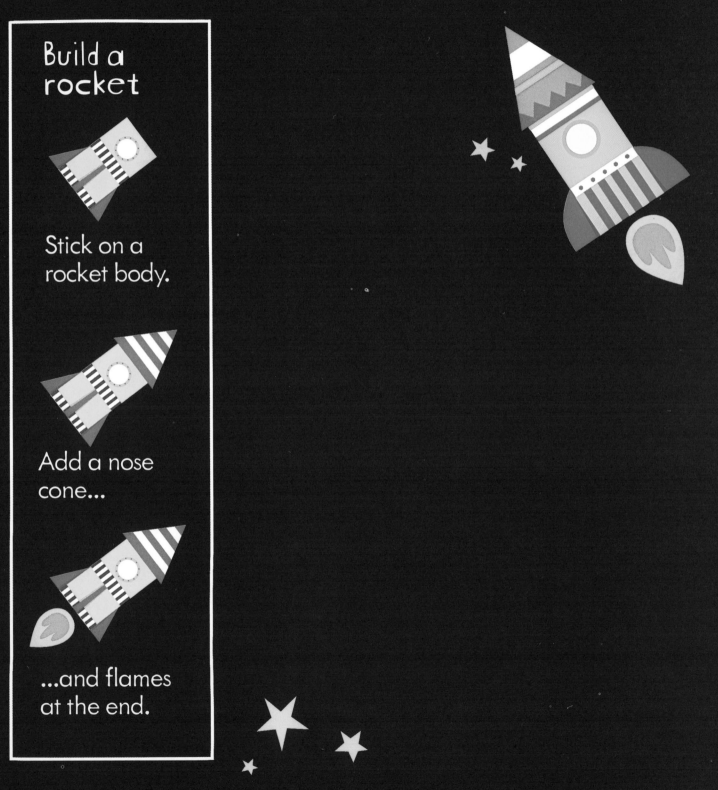

Build a rocket

Stick on a rocket body.

Add a nose cone...

...and flames at the end.

Add star and
planet stickers
in the sky, too.

Fill the planet with aliens. Stick different
bodies and heads together.

53

Vacation hotel

Can you spot ten differences between this picture...

...and this one? Circle each difference.

Travel fun

Fill in the shapes. Each number stands for a different color.

1 =
2 =
3 =
4 =
5 =

Find the passenger stickers on the sticker pages. Then, stick each one on top of the window it matches.

Usborne Activity Books

Route 123

Add the pigeon stickers, too.

Park life

Can you spot two identical birds in the tree?

How to draw a duck

Draw a circle for its head.

Add a body and a wing.

Then, give it a beak and an eye.

Draw more ducks on the pond and color them in.

Which girl is Lily? Look at the picture and read the clues, then circle her.

- Lily is sitting down.
- She has long hair.
- She is wearing sunglasses.

Can you find Hugh, too?

- Hugh has dark hair.
- He isn't wearing shoes.
- He is playing with a toy.

Vacation pics

Fill this vacation photo album with
the stickers from the sticker pages.
Match each one to its label.

On the beach

Rock climbing

Ice cream

Swimming

At the zoo

My new friends

Answers

4–5 Departures

- luggage carts
- **sleeping passengers**
- woman putting on her boots
- girl playing with car
- **striped suitcases**
- boy playing with plane
- girl taking photos

8–9 On the beach

This seagull only has one leg.

10–11 Snowy slopes

There are 7 people skiing and 4 people snowboarding.

There are 7 animals to spot.

12–13 Making camp

Stick the red tent here.

This RV's wipers are pointing in a different direction.

16–17 At the market

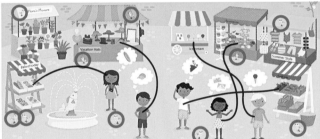

There are 10 pigeons in the picture.

18–19 Making a splash

Square c is missing from the puzzle.

There are 6 yellow ducks.

20–21 Town travel

22-23 Up in the air

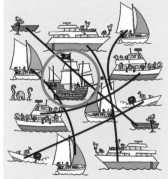

- ⚪ spotted hot-air balloons
- ⚪ jumbo jet
- ⚫ striped planes
- ⚪ plane with 2 pilots
- ⚪ helicopters
- ⚪ birds that aren't flying

24-25 At sea

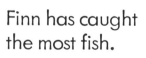

Finn has caught the most fish.

crab

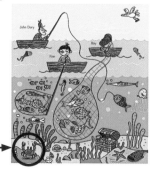

26-27 Packing

Harry's sunglasses are missing.

The red car is going to the train station.
The green car is going to the airport.
The blue car is going to the bus station.

28-29 Platform puzzles

--- This is Jack.

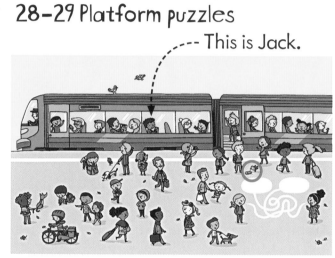

⚪ Simon's ticket

I'm Alex.

I'm Jenny.

30-31 Picture postcards

62

34–35 Pedal power

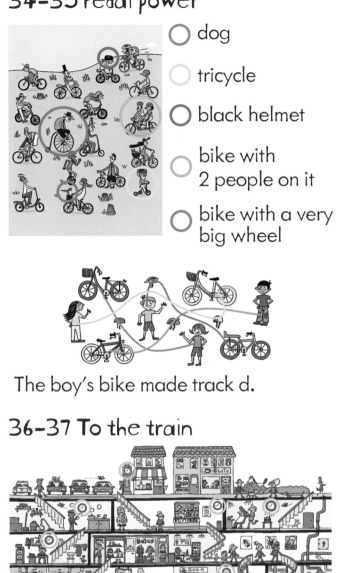

- ○ dog
- ○ tricycle
- ○ black helmet
- ○ bike with 2 people on it
- ○ bike with a very big wheel

The boy's bike made track d.

36–37 To the train

- ○ There are 6 clocks.

38–39 Harbor view

- ○ submarine

40–41 Airport arrivals

42–43 Tidepool hunt

- ○ 4 🐟
- ○ 5 🦀
- ○ 7 ⭐
- ○ 3 🪸
- ○ 6 🥅
- ○ 7 🪣
- ○ 1 🦐
- ○ 6 🐦

63

44-45 On the move

There are 5 red cars and 4 blue cars in the rows.

46-47 Time to eat

48-49 Where in the world?

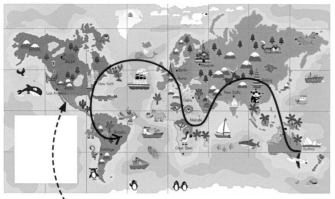

Anna is in this square.

50-51 On safari

Sophie took photo c.

This zebra is missing a stripe.

You should number the giraffes from left to right: 4, 2, 3, 1, 5

54-55 Vacation hotel

58-59 Park life

These birds are identical.

I'm Hugh.

I'm Lily.

First published in 2013 by Usborne Publishing Ltd., Usborne House, 83-85 Saffron Hill, London EC1N 8RT, England. www.usborne.com © 2013 Usborne Publishing Ltd.
The name Usborne and the devices are Trade Marks of Usborne Publishing Ltd. All rights reserved. No part of this publication may be reproduced, stored in a retrieval system or transmitted in any form or by any means, electronic, mechanical, photocopying, recording or otherwise without the prior permission of the publisher. AE.
First published in America in 2013. Printed in Dubai, UAE.